THE
MARINA

FIRST EDITION
Published in 2022

Author: Nathan Lyle Cunningham
www.YouTube.com/NathanLyleOfficial
www.Twitter.com/NathanLyle

ISBN: 978-1-7343061-4-9

Library of Congress in Publication Data

Category: Action, Adventure, Sci-Fi, Comic

Library of Congress Cataloging-in-Publication Data

Publishing Consultant & Designer: Eli Blyden | EliTheBookGuy.com

Printed & Published in the United States of America

TABLE OF CONTENTS

THE
MARINA

BY NATHAN LYLE CUNNINGHAM

THE MARINA

The mews of herring gulls gathering for their morning feast. The smell of salt filling the air with every wave that crashes down. Those are the familiar markers you can look forward to every morning when you wake up in the coastal city of Morning Dew, the Las Vegas of southern Maine.

Morning Dew, named after the ship that brought the first settlers, has been around since the 1600s. There's never less than two million people in the city at any one time. Less than 200,000 of them are legally considered permanent residents. Approximately 170,000 of them were born there. Nearly 120,000 of them will die without ever stepping a single foot beyond the city boundaries.

In the summer of 1988 Geoffrey, a 17 year old Caucasian boy just under six feet tall with short, dirty blonde hair, has spent his entire life fearing that he would be a member of that final group. His mother is the city's greatest disappointment. They don't hate her. Quite the opposite. They treat her like the disabled step-child. Everyone goes out of their way to keep her housed, fed and, whenever possible, away from drugs.

She gave birth to Geoffrey when she was 14, a month before she was supposed to start high school. The majority of adults Geoffrey interacts with treat him like a nephew. They go out of their way to ease his life. When the NES was released he was gifted three of them for Christmas. That love for him is the reason why Geoffrey was able to avoid some legal hurdles and start working at The Marina three years ago.

In Morning Dew there are four main attractions that keep drawing in the tourist and earning enough money that the city can avoid being purchased by a Russian oligarch. Most unique amongst those attractions is The Marina, a coastal water park a few miles east of the harbor.

Geoffrey never has trouble waking up in the morning. His alarm is beams of sunlight poking through the blinds to hit him right in the eyes. He jumps out of bed, takes a quick shower then throws on some fresh clothes. He walks to his mom's room and tentatively pushes the door open.

He lets out a heavy sigh at the sight of her passed out face down on the bed. She has long black hair which hasn't been cut since before he was born. Today it's spread out like a fan covering her entire upper body. Her shoes are still on. Geoffrey walks in and as he's taking them off he notices a stain on the bed.

"Ugh, mom. Not again."

Geoff goes to the kitchen where he cooks sausage, scrambled eggs and toast. He splits them evenly between two plates and covers one of the plates with plastic wrap. He pours himself a glass of orange juice then takes his food to the table and sits down to eat while reading the paper.

Once he finishes he rinses his plate and leaves it in the sink. He grabs a backpack that's resting by the door, tosses it over his shoulders and walks outside. He lifts the bike out of the grass on his front lawn, turns on his Walkman and listens to Rick Astley as he rides through the city with the wind in his face, his hair flowing behind him, taking in the fresh air.

He soars past the edge of town and pedals down an open road until he's greeted by a big blue sign with the words *The Marina* in bold white letters alongside pictures of a dolphin and a school of fish. As Geoffrey approaches the security guard presses the button and the gate starts sliding open.

"Morning Gary."

"Morning Geoff. You have a great day."

"Thanks. You too."

Geoffrey likes to slow down as he rides through the park. The longer he works there the more it feels like home. There's only one roller coaster but it has two loops. A playground for the kids that includes things like a mini waterfall and metal dolphins and whales on springs. Plus carnival row, a line of booths where you can play games and buy junk food.

One of the central attractions is the aquarium; a two story high building full of tanks holding various fish from around the world. Some of them garden variety, others rare and exotic. Though two stories high the building has only one floor. If you wish to view the higher tanks you need to climb on of the many ladders scattered along the walls and walk across the metal platforms.

Geoffrey rides to the back of the park where the staff building is. The front half of the building is an infirmary.

Geoffrey rides to the back of the building. The door has an electronic lock. He punches in the code and opens the door to a large hallway. The walls are lined with lockers. Once inside he puts his bike on a rack off to the side. There are a handful of people in the room but Geoffrey's eyes lock onto one.

Maria. Part black, part Latina, part Native. This girl has a little bit of everything sprinkled in there. She's 26 years old, 5'5 with caramel skin, brown eyes, curly black hair that bounces down her shoulders. Thick luscious lips that look soft like pillows.

She moved from Louisiana five years earlier. When Geoffrey first started the job Maria was the one who trained him. The moment he met her his heart stopped. Even though he's spent the last three years obsessed with her he knows dating has never been a realistic possibility. She sees him more like a little brother.

Still, every time she's near him his knees get weak and his heart beats out of his chest. The mere thought of her intoxicates him. When he approaches her she's standing in front of her open locker. There's a large mirror covering the interior of the door. She's applying a layer of gloss to her lips.

"Good Morning Maria."

"Mornin' Geoff."

"You look lovely as usual."

"Flattery will get you everywhere."

She finishes applying her makeup and ties her hair up in a bun.

"So where they got you stationed today?"

"Tours. You?"

"Tickets in the morning, concessions in the afternoon."

"It's better than janitorial."

"If they ever put me on that again I'm quitting."

"No you're not."

She slams her locker shut.

"You wouldn't leave me here by myself."

As she walks past him she gently pats his shoulder. He hides his face because he knows he's blushing so hard he'd make Rudolph jealous. He walks to the changing rooms in back where he throws on his uniform. Then he tosses his bag in a locker and heads to the front of the park.

There's a row of turnstiles with security gaurs posted on either side. People with season passes stroll right on through. The rest stop by the ticket booth where Geoffrey is posted.

It's a fairly normal day for Geoffrey…with the exception of a few strange interactions. There's a middle aged man wearing a beige five-piece suit and pink sunglasses. He also has a navy blue trench coat draped over his shoulders and a matching fedora on his head. The man approaches the booth and just stands there staring at Geoffrey with a blank expression.

"It's ten bucks for an adult ticket."

The man hands Geoffrey a one hundred dollar bill. Geoffrey slides a ticket over to the man then opens the register to get some change. The man doesn't wait for his change. He just grabs the ticket and walks to the gate leaving Geoffrey perplexed.

Immediately after that man leaves a teenage boy, maybe a year or two younger than Geoffrey, walks up to the gate. He has a thin frame, light brown skin and black dreadlocks poking out from underneath the Celtics hat. He looks dressed to play with sandals, red swim trunks and a t-shirt with a picture of a dolphin on it. There's a silver chain on his neck with a locket hanging from it.

When the kid steps to the gate he sees Geoffrey and his jaw drops. The boy just stands there silently staring at Geoffrey with wide eyes.

"You okay kid?"

No response. Geoffrey snaps his fingers a few times.

"Helloooooo?"

The kid shakes his head.

"Um….how much?"

"You under 15?"

"Uh, yeah."

"Seven bucks."

The kid pulls out a small wallet. He hands Geoffrey a five dollar bill and two ones. Geoffrey hands the kid a ticket and says "Have a good day." The kid says "You too," and backs away from the gate, still staring Geoffrey down.

The exchange was unusual, but not as unnerving as the guy wearing a suit. Geoffrey finishes the rest of his shift then heads out for his lunch break. Most employees will just grab something from the concession stands then take a nap in the breakroom. Geoffrey wants to spend his break with Maria. He asks another employee if they know where she is.

"Last I saw she was headed to The Cove."

The Cove is The Marina's main attraction. It cost the city millions of dollars to make and earned that money back in the first few months of opening. They dug a giant hole 20 feet into the ground, just a couple feet away from the ocean. In that room they built a stainless steel floor and three stainless steel walls. The fourth wall, the one closest to the water, was made of ten inch thick ballistic glass. Then they smashed the natural stone wall.

Most people take the elevator down. Some people took the stairs but not many. You can spend hours in that room just staring into the ocean. Depending on the season there are times when you can spend the entire day down there and not see a single creature. Other times you can see schools of fish or dolphins and whales. There's always at least one Marine Biologist in the room just in case someone has questions.

When Geoffrey steps out of the elevator most of the people in the room are standing by the glass watching a few fish swim around while the biologist explains their genecology and list some fun facts. Geoffrey notices that those two weirdos from earlier are both down there. The man with the suit is mixed in with the crowd while the kid with the dreadlocks is in the back of the room glaring at the man in the suit. Geoffrey walks over to Maria who's explaining to a small group of people how the cove was built. When Maria sees Geoffrey she smiles and excuses herself.

"Hey. You on break?"

"Yeah. I was, you know, kinda wonderin' if ya wanted to grab a bite together or something?"

"As long as it's just two coworkers eating lunch and not something more."

Geoffrey nodded.

"Yeah. Sure. Of course that's what I mean."

"Well then, I'd love to."

The man in the suit turns around and walks to the elevators. Before stepping on he looks at the kid with the dreads and smiles. The kid with dreads seems spooked by that. A tourist says "what's that?" and everyone turns to see a large object in the water that seems to be headed straight for them.

"Is that a shark?"

"I never seen one a those in real life."

The biologist adjust his glasses and presses his nose against the glass.

"That's not just any shark. Note the coloration and the round fins. That is an Oceanic Whitetip shark."

"Are they rare?"

"I would never expect to see one here. They prefer warmer waters and open ocean. So to see one this far north and this close to the shore is highly unlikely."

As it gets closer and closer they see how tremendous it is.

"That thing is huge."

"You rarely see them grow past ten feet but the largest specimens ever caught were 13 feet and 370 pounds. However, this one seems like it might be well past 20 feet."

The shark stops just inches in front of the glass. It almost feels like the creature is peering at them through the glass. The shark turns around and as it swims away everyone notices an identical shark swimming towards the glass.

"Extraordinary. Seeing just one of these sharks is unbelievable. This is truly a once in a lifetime event."

As the shark gets closer Geoffrey notices something. Unlike the first shark this one isn't slowing down. It rams the glass with enough force that the entire room shakes. Some ocean water splashes in from over the glass.

Everyone's looking at each other with fear and confusion. One person makes the suggestion that the second shark must be blind. Then, as the second shark moves away, the first shark swims straight towards them. It slams into the glass, shaking the walls and floor and splashing more water into the room.

People are getting knocked off their feet. As Geoffrey pushes himself up he touches something with his hand. It's small, sharp and jagged. He picks it up and sees that it's clear. His eyes go wide when he realizes what he's holding. He looks up and sees the sharks both backing away from the glass.

"Evacuate!"

Everyone stares at Geoffrey as he jumps to his feet.

"We need to get everyone up the stairs. Now!"

The employees start leading the visitors towards the staircase. A small crowd of people heads for the elevators but Maria runs to cut them off.

"In emergency situations the elevators might shut down and you could end up trapped. Please take the stairs."

"Brace for impact!"

The sharks both ram into the glass knocking everyone in the room off their feet. Cracks are spreading through the glass.

"Everybody move! Go! Go!"

Everyone is on their feet and running for their lives. They each scramble up the stairs as quickly as their legs will take them. As the cracks grow water leaks in. It only takes a few seconds for the people on the ground to be ankle deep in water. A few seconds later it's up to their knees.

Once the last of the customers is on the stairs the employees begin climbing. Geoffrey is right behind Maria. The water is rising quicker than they can climb. The people at the very bottom are swimming. Then…the sharks slam into the glass again.

The glass shatters. Pieces of it fly out and impale a couple of the people climbing. The water rushes in, completely submerging the staircase. Geoffrey grabs the railing and clings for dear life.

As the initial surge subsides Geoffrey opens his eyes and sees some of his coworkers being swept out by the current. The sharks are gobbling them up one by one. Geoffrey looks around until he locates Maria. She lost consciousness and the current is pulling her towards the open ocean.

Geoffrey lets go of the railing and swims with the current, avoiding broken glass along the way until he reaches Maria.

He grabs her and rises to the surface where he takes a huge breath. He desperately swims back to the shore as quickly as his body will move.

When he reaches the shore Geoffrey holds Maria up and the kid with the dreads grabs her and pulls her up. Geoffrey puts his hands on solid ground and pushes himself up. As he puts one leg on dry land a shark's head burst out of the water and bites down on Geoffrey's other leg.

Geoffrey lets out a huge scream as the shark yanks him back under water. The shark keeps pulling him deeper. Geoffrey's leg is bleeding and his lungs are filling with water. Just before he passes out Geoffrey sees the other shark swimming towards him with its jaw open wide.

When Geoffrey opens his eyes he's staring at a white ceiling. A lightbulb immediately in view is irritating him. He tries to sit up but his entire body is sore. A hand touches his shoulder. He looks up and sees Maria sitting by his bedside.

"Where am I?"

"The infirmary."

"What? How?"

"Some kid jumped in and grabbed you."

"Kid? What kid?"

"Um, he looked about 15. Black. Dreadlocks."

"Celtics hat and a dolphin shirt?"

"Yeah. How'd you know?"

"I gave him his ticket this morning."

"Good thing you did. He ended up saving your life."

"But…how? There were two sharks."

"No one knows. He jumped into the water, pulled you out, then ran away. No one's seen him since."

She leans forward and kisses his cheek.

"I really don't care. I'm just glad you're ok."

Geoffrey blushes.

"I just realized I haven't asked you how you are."

"Better than you. I got mouth to mouth and jumped right back up. You were unconscious and gushing blood.

The memory of the shark suddenly pops into his head. Geoffrey tosses the blanket off and sees the lower half of his right leg covered in gauze.

"It's actually not too bad. The teeth didn't go through your leg. Your leg got stuck in between the teeth. Your bones are cracked, there's some muscle damage and you lost a lot of blood. But for the most part you should be fine."

"Wow. Lucky break."

"They're still worried about infection. They want you to go to a hospital and get it checked out."

"I can't skip work."

"Well guess what, turns out getting attacked by a shark earns you a vacation."

She rises to her feet and rustles his hair.

"Enjoy your week off."

As she walks out the door Geoffrey is trying to sort through his feelings. He's over the moon about that kiss, confused about the boy with the dreads, worried about his leg and anxious about the weirdness of it all. That's when a nurse walks over to Geoffrey.

"Have you tried standing up?"

"Uh, not yet."

"You're on painkillers so it should be ok to move. It might sting a little bit but you should be alright. Your leg didn't break but it will if you push yourself too much."

When Geoffrey first puts weight on his leg there is a stinging pain. He powers through it and every step he takes hurts less and less till the pain has subsided completely.

"The pain is still there but once the adrenaline starts pumping it becomes easier to ignore. You should still take it easy."

"I'll keep that in mind."

"I'd love to keep you but you know the rules. I have to keep the beds clear whenever possible."

"I'm fine. Don't worry about me."

Geoffrey walks back to the locker rooms. Along the way every person he bumps into tells him how happy they are to see he's ok. He grabs his backpack out of the locker and walks to the changing room. He takes off his work uniform, throws it in a plastic grocery bag and ties it shut, then puts his normal clothes back on and shoves the plastic bag in his backpack.

He goes to the back door and grabs his bike. The moment he opens the door there's a crowd of people holding cameras, lights and microphones. There's a line of cops holding back the horde. One of the cops walks up to Geoffrey and says "I'm here to escort you safely out of the park."

As the cop leads Geoffrey through the crowd the people keep pointing their cameras and microphones, pestering him incessantly. Then, a screech cuts through the air and everyone turns their heads to see the rollercoaster has stopped upside down in the middle of a loop. The entire crowd moves in that direction while Geoffrey stands there stunned.

The reporters and cops are all asking what's going on. No one knows for sure why it happened. The ride was going full speed when it suddenly stopped on a dime. The violent jerk knocked a few people unconscious. A few riders were flung so hard that their seatbelts snapped off and now they're clinging to the safety bars for dear life.

The cops call dispatch and ask for ambulances and firetrucks. The one in charge says to set up a perimeter so the cops start pushing the reporters back. A couple of them grab some yellow tape. Someone screams and everyone looks up in time to see a man lose his grip and fall to his death, splattering against the ground.

Some of the reporters and cameramen try to rush forward. The cops struggle to hold them back. Geoff looks at the rollercoaster. Those people are husbands and wives, brothers and sisters, sons and daughters. The longer everyone stands there waiting the less survivors there will be.

With his heart ready to beat right through his sternum Geoffrey lets his bike fall to the ground and drops his backpack on top of it. He runs. Once he reaches the food stands he turns and runs through the playground. He jumps over the coaster's back gate and runs to the loading platform.

"Hey! There's someone going up!"

"Stop! It's too dangerous!"

Geoffrey runs up the stairs to the rails. Then he runs along the rails until he reaches the loop.

"Get down from there!"

"Be careful Geoff!"

Geoffrey slowly walks up the incline, staying close to the edge. Nearly halfway up the slope becomes so steep he can barely keep himself from sliding down. He reaches his arms over to grab the edge of the planks. While gripping them tightly he slides one foot over and moves an arm to the other side.

After struggling to pull his entire body over he's drenched with sweat and on the verge of hyperventilating so he takes a moment to catch his breath before he starts crawling towards the top. As the incline smooths Geoffrey gets back on his feet and runs to where the cars stopped. He lays on his stomach and pokes his head over the edge.

"Is everyone ok?"

"No!"

"Help us! Please!"

"I'm so scared."

"Everyone stay calm. I'm gonna get you out."

"Hurry!"

Geoffrey is examining the scene, wondering how he can get down there in the first place, much less come back up carrying someone.

"You need some help?"

Geoffrey turns around and sees the kid with the dreadlocks standing behind him.

"How did you get up here?"

"I was right behind you the whole time."

Geoffrey doesn't buy it. He feels like he would've noticed a black guy chasing him up a roller coaster. Then again, he was very focused on not falling."

"How about I hold your legs while you slide down and grab people?"

"Can you hold my weight?"

"I'm stronger than I look."

Geoffrey is hesitant. Can he really trust a total stranger with his life? Well, it's what he's about to ask of the people below. Geoffrey nods. The kid bends down grabbing Geoffrey by the legs as Geoffrey slowly slides his body over the edge.

The kid holds Geoffrey's ankles pressed against the edge of the boards. The boy is straining but he manages to hold Geoffrey steady. Geoffrey's head pokes over the top of the first car. There's a mother with one arm wrapped around her unconscious son, holding him in place. Her other arm is wrapped around the safety bar.

"Are you two alright?"

"I'm ok. But he hit his head."

Geoffrey sees the young boy is bleeding from a cut on his forehead. He reaches an arm out.

"Pass him to me."

She shakes her head.

"I promise I won't drop him."

She shakes her head again.

"He's safe with me. I won't let him fall."

Geoffrey is feeling somewhat discouraged. He hears a fearful shout from the next car over. A man is hanging from the safety bar by only the grip of his fingers. He's slipping down. Geoffrey waves at the kid holding him.

The kid is taking slow, gentle steps over while Geoffrey steadies himself against the side of the cars. Once he's gotten close enough Geoffrey grabs the safety bar with one hand and stretches out with the other.

"Grab my hand!"

"I can't! It's too far!"

"You have to try!"

The guy looks down below then back at Geoffrey. He reaches his off arm back up and grabs the safety bar. Hand over hand the man pulls himself until he's close enough to reach out for Geoffrey's right hand.

Their fingers touch. The man stretches a little further and those fingers lock. Geoffrey takes his left hand off the bar and grabs the guy's wrist. Then moves his right hand down to hold the man's forearm.

"You have to let go."

The man nods his head then closes his eyes and releases his grip on the bar. Geoffrey is squeezing the man's wrist as he dangles. The extra strain is a bit much for the kid with the dreads.

"Get him steady! My shoulders are about to pop off!"

Geoffrey starts yanking the man up till their faces are almost touching.

"You're gonna have to climb me."

The man nods then reaches his left hand up to grab Geoffrey's right armpit. Geoffrey lets go of the man's hand. The man reaches his right arm up and throws it around Geoffrey's abdomen. The kid with the dreads is struggling to hold on. His hands are sliding up Geoffrey's legs into his shoes.

"Hurry!"

The man grabs onto Geoffrey's belt. He gives one big yank, accidently giving Geoffrey a wedgie, and pulls his right hand up to grab the edge of the boards between the other kid's feet. He raises he left arm and looks at the kid.

"You wanna give me a hand?"

"I can barely hold this guy."

"Maybe I can help?"

The kid with the dreads turns his head and sees a cop standing next to him. The cop kneels down so he can grab the man's arm. As the cop is pulling the man up one of Geoffrey's coworkers reaches down and grabs the man as well. Once that man is safe the coworker grabs Geoffrey and helps pull him back up.

Geoffrey sits on top of the roller coaster and looks around. A handful of cops and his coworkers all ascended the roller coaster chasing after him and are copying his example. All of the riders are being evacuated from the train cars and safely escorted back down to the ground. A cop walks over to Geoffrey and extends his hand.

"Let's get you outta here."

Geoffrey shakes his head.

"Listen, ya did good kid. But how 'bout you leave the rest to us?"

"I have a promise to keep. I'm going back down."

The cop looks at Geoffrey like he's crazy, then he lies flat on the edge of the coaster.

"I'll hoist you down."

Geoffrey lies next to the cop and as he slowly crawls down the cop is keeping a firm grip on Geoffrey's right leg. Once Geoffrey has gone mostly over the tracks the cops is firmly gripping each ankle. Geoffrey pokes his head over the top of the car and sees the woman squeezing her eyes shut, still desperately clutching her boy. She's crying. Geoffrey grabs onto the safety bar and looks up at the cop.

"Let me go."

The look on his face says 'no way in hell' but to even his own shock he releases his grip and Geoffrey's legs swing down. He swings his legs up and wraps them around the safety bar. He reaches an arm out and taps the woman on the shoulder. She opens her eyes and looks at him.

"Pass him to me."

She shakes her head.

"I promise I won't drop him."

She shakes her head again.

"Look…I know you're scared. And you're a mom. You think no one can protect your kid as well as you can. But you've been hanging upside down for a long time. You're getting woozy aren't you? Pretty soon you'll lose consciousness and you won't be able to hold yourself in place, much less your son, and you'll both fall. You're gonna have to trust me."

She stares at him for a few seconds before nodding her head. She holds her son with both hands and holds him out towards Geoffrey. Geoffrey double checks his legs to make sure he's stable before taking his hands off the bar. He reaches out and pulls the boy into his arms.

"I got the kid! Send someone down!"

One of Geoffrey's taller coworkers volunteers so the cop lowers that guy down. Geoffrey gently passes the boy to him and a couple of cops pull the coworker up. Geoffrey turns back to the woman and extends his arms. She nods. As she's unbuckling herself they hear a noise. Before anyone can ask what that noise was the cars start moving again.

Geoffrey and the woman cling to the safety bar for dear life as the cars careen out of control down the track. There's chaos down below. There were people still on the track when the cars started moving and they had to leap to the ground. Employees are at the controls trying to figure out any kind of explanation.

The cars are headed for a sharp turn. At this speed they might derail. Suddenly, the kid with the dreadlocks lands on the front of the car. The wind knocks his hat off and is blowing his hair everywhere. Purple bolts of electricity shoot out of his hands and surge through the car till it comes to a complete stop.

Geoffrey is struggling to catch his breath. He raises his head to see the kid standing on the front of the train pushing the braids from his face. Geoffrey can't wrap his head around everything that's happened today…but this kid definitely has something to do with it.

The kid stares silently at Geffrey for a few seconds. Then he notices cops and reporters rushing in their direction. The kid winks at Geoffrey then leaps off the track. He shoots more electricity out of his hands to slow his descent and he lands softly. The moment his feet touch the ground he's running away as fast as he can.

After asking if she's ok, Geoffrey helps the woman out of her seat and walks with her back down to the ground. A doctor examines Geoffrey. He didn't even notice his mouth was bleeding. His face hit the safety bar and he chipped a tooth. As the police are escorting him back to the staff building the reporters keep asking him questions. The police tell Geoffrey to just keep his head down and don't say anything.

Most of the employees hide out in the staff building while the cops clear the place out. After a few hours the manager walks in. He says the owner was contacted and informed that due to safety concerns The Marina will be shut down indefinitely.

"What does indefinitely mean?"

"It means it'll open when it opens."

"If it ever opens again."

The manager assures them that The Marina will open again. They just need a month or two to double check all their equipment and safety procedures. Once they can ensure successful operations they will start reaching out to the employees to return. For now, everyone starts clearing out their lockers. As Geoff finishes emptying his locker a male coworker comes over and starts emptying Maria's locker.

"Where's Maria?"

"She left before the coaster went haywire. Cops wouldn't let her back in. We live in the same neighborhood so I'm gonna drop her stuff off."

"Ok. Tell her I said have a good summer and I'll see her next year."

"Will do."

Geoffrey walks out the door and jumps on his bike. As he rides home he takes time to enjoy the moon. He wishes he didn't live in a big city. There are stars in the sky but he knows there would be far more visible with less light pollution.

He gets home and drops his bike on the grass. When he opens the door he's shocked to see the kid with the dreadlocks sitting at the table. He's got a glass of water and a saucer with one slice of bread on it sitting in front of him. When Geoffrey slams the door shut the kid turns his head to face him.

"Welcome home."

Geoffrey drops his backpack.

"Who are you and how the fuck did you get in my house?"

"My name is Travis. The door was sitting wide open."

Geoffrey rolls his eyes.

"God dammit mom."

 Geoffrey walks to the table and sits opposite Travis.

"Well, Travis, Why are you here? And how are you here? Did you know where I live? How? Why me? And what for?"

Travis takes a sip from his glass.

"Tell me Geoffrey…do you believe in magic?"

"Of course not."

Travis points at the bread and purple electricity shoots out of his finger toasting the bread.

"Neither do I."

Travis lifts up the slice of toast. Steam is rising from it as he moves it to his mouth. There's a familiar crunch as Travis sinks his teeth into the bread. Crumbs fall from his mouth with each chew.

"Do you know anything about chaos theory?"

"No."

"Would you like to?"

"I'd like to know why you're in my house. And what you know about all the weird shit that happened today. And why you're able to shoot lightening."

"I can explain all of it. But you're far more likely to understand it if I explain chaos theory first."

"Well explain it to me then."

"You want the dictionary definition?"

"I've never been that great at school so try to dumb it down for me."

"Well, the simplest way to explain it is…everything that happens, affects everything else that happens."

"That seems pretty self-explanatory."

"Ok. That was too oversimplified. Let me try again."

He clears his throat and takes a sip of water.

"Have you ever heard of the butterfly effect?"

"Not at all."

"It's the underlying principal of chaos. One small change can lead to drastically different results. A butterfly flaps its wings in China and you get a hurricane in Texas instead of sunshine."

"How is that even possible?"

"Because everything in the universe is connected. The tiniest change here can start a chain reaction that leads to monumental changes over there."

"Chaos theory."

"Now, what do you think time is?"

"Time?"

"Explain it to me."

"Time, it's…you know…seconds, minutes, hours, days."

"But what if I didn't know what any of those words meant? How would you explain to me what time is?"

"I'm obviously never gonna give the right answer so why don't you just tell me what you want me to know?"

"Time doesn't exist."

"What?"

"Time isn't real. It doesn't exist."

"The hell are you talking about? Of course it exist."

"How do you know?"

"Because…things change. We get older, we die."

"Exactly. Time is a concept of human perception. It was created as a way of explaining why our bodies keep growing. Why we die. Why fruit ripens and decays."

Travis drops the piece of toast in the middle of the table.

"The biggest mistake people make is thinking that time is a thing that moves while they stand still."

As Travis says this he slowly waves the plate over the toast.

"But the truth is, what you know as time is a static fabric."

Travis pulls the toast back and puts the plate in the middle of the table. Then he slowly waves the toast over the plate.

"Time does not move. We move through it."

Travis rips the toast into eight smaller pieces and lines them up in a row.

"Truth is, everything that can happen has already happened. And everything that's already happened will continue happening eternally. The world does not change. The decisions we make change which world our conscious minds are allowed to perceive."

Travis slides a piece of toast towards Geoffrey.

"One day a coworker offers to let your mom stay at her place."

Travis slides another piece of toast towards Geoffrey.

"She doesn't call to tell you she won't be coming home tonight. So you stay up late worrying about her."

Travis slides another piece of toast.

"You wake up late and rush to school."

He slides another piece of toast.

"Because you were in a hurry to get to class you didn't pay attention and bumped into a girl."

He slides another piece of toast.

"Three years later you two say I love you for the first time."

He slides another piece of toast.

"Years after that you get married."

He slides another piece of toast.

"Years after that she gives birth to your son."

Travis slides the final piece of toast over to Geoffrey.

"Years later your son grows up to cure cancer or start World War 3. No one knows for sure yet."

Travis uses his hand to slide all but one piece of toast back to himself.

"But there are infinite universes where you never meet that girl in the first place. Because your mom came home. Or because she at least called to let you know she would be staying somewhere else. You went to bed at a decent hour. The next day at school you calmly walked past that girl, barely even noticing she was there."

Travis picks up one of the toasted dots and pops it in his mouth.

"There are parallel universes where you don't exist. Your mom never met the guy that got her pregnant. She didn't have her first child till six years later when she was happily married. It was a beautiful girl named Tiffany.

There are versions of this world where The United States never existed. Columbus actually made it to North America and Spain colonized the new world instead of Britain. There are versions of Maine where Morning Dew doesn't exist. In this world Maine doesn't have Bangor or Portland."

"Portland? Isn't that in Oregon?"

"There are 30 states with a city called Springfield. That's why The Simpsons is set there."

"The Simpsons? What's that?"

"You'll find out soon."

Travis takes a sip of water. Geoffrey rises to his feet and starts pacing.

"OK...Let's just say that everything you've just told me is true, and that I actually understood any of it, what does all this have to do with me?"

"An external force has entered this time stream and altered the natural course of events. My job is to stop him."

"Him...The man in the suit?"

Travis nods.

"We used to work together. He decided he was tired of following the rules. Now he jumps from one universe to the next wreaking havoc."

"So you knew he was here to cause trouble and you didn't stop him?"

"Because I'm still following the rules. I'm supposed to lay low and avoid detection. Too much tampering can have serious ramifications."

"People died while you were laying low!"

"And I can't change that. But if you help me, we can stop many more deaths from happening."

Geoffrey leans back against a wall and rubs both hands over his face before looking back to Travis.

"What do you want from me?"

"For now, I just need you to get me back into that park."

Geoffrey folds his arms and stares at the ground for a few seconds while he contemplates. Then he lets out a soft sigh.

"OK. I'll do it."

Geoffrey starts walking towards his room.

"Where you goin?"

"Gonna take a quick shower then pass out. Wake me up in 3 hours."

"Sure thing."

Geoffrey jumps in the shower for 25 minutes to thoroughly wash the stench of the day off his body. Then he dries himself off, throws on some pajamas and flops down in bed. He doesn't even bother crawling under the covers. Just lays down and closes his eyes. Next thing he knows he's being nudged. Geoffrey opens one eye and turns his head to see Travis standing over him.

"It's time."

Geoffrey groans as he crawls out of bed, stretches out his arms and pops his neck. As he's throwing on clean clothes he explains the plan to Travis.

"The best time to sneak in is the middle of the night. There's minimal security working the graveyard shift so that's when you can most easily maneuver around undetected."

Geoffrey puts on his shoes then he and Travis head outside. Geoffrey picks his bike off the ground.

"How are you getting there?"

Travis walks to the curb where Geoffrey's mom parked the car. He touches the hood and sparks shoot out of his hands. The car starts and Travis opens the driver side door.

"You coming?"

Geoffrey drops the bike and walks to the car.

"Are you even old enough to drive?"

"I don't exist in the corporeal universe and I'm therefore not bound by the rules of time."

They both get in the car and buckle up.

"But if you count all the hours that I've lived since I began this lifestyle…I'm 76."

As Travis drives Geoffrey gives him directions. Travis is confused when they end up at the port.

"The best place to sneak in is through the ocean."

They both get out of the car and Travis follows Geoffrey as he runs to the ocean and dives in. Together they swim towards The Marina. They enter through the former Cove and climb the steps up. Geoffrey was right. Not a single guard in sight.

"What makes you so sure that guy will be here?"

"I'm not. But earlier today he came here for a reason. I'm banking on the hope that the reason still exist."

They walk through The Marina unimpeded for the most part. There was one close call with a security guard as they passed through carnival alley but they ducked into a booth until she passed. They rose up just in time to see the man in the suit walking into the aquarium. They run for him. The moment they burst in the door Travis yells at the man.

"Why did you betray us Saenz?"

Saenz chuckles then turns around.

"Don't you ever get tired of following those stupid rules? Do you even know what you're fighting for?"

"Yes."

Travis fires electricity from his hands. It hits Saenz, sending him flying across the room. He bumps into some glass, cracking it, then crumples to the ground. Saenz rises to his feet. He holds up his hand and the glass behind him shatters. The water pours out. The fish are flopping on the ground. The shards of glass are floating around Saenz's head.

Saenz points his hand forward and the shards of glass fly towards Geoffrey and Travis. Travis holds his hands out and bolts of electricity fly out of his fingers bursting all the shards. Saenz raises both his hands and every glass in the building shatters. As water is filling the floor Saenz claps his hands in front of him.

All the shards of glass, as well as octopus, swordfish and all kinds of marine life, go flying towards Geffrey and Travis.

Travis keeps spinning around, constantly firing off electricity. He's able to hit every fish but little shards of glass keep sneaking through leavings tiny cuts all over his face and body.

Geoffrey notices that Saenz is ignoring him and focusing all his attacks on Travis. So he runs for Saenz. As he approaches the water on the floor gathers and rises up into a fist which punches Geoffrey into a wall. Then the fist flies across the room towards Travis.

Travis blast the fist with electricity, evaporating it. With Travis distracted more shards of glass make it to him. He's got cuts all over his face, arms, legs and abdomen. By this point he's got more cuts than skin. He falls to his knees huffing and puffing, blood dripping from every section of his body. All the glass, water and fish fall harmlessly to the ground and Saenz calmly walks over to Travis.

"Did you really think you could beat me?"

Travis shakes his head.

"No…"

Travis looks up at Saenz with a smile.

"…not me."

Geoffrey stabs a swordfish into Saenz's back. The bill goes straight through Saenz's heart. Saenz collapses face down in a puddle. Blood is oozing out of him. Geoffrey holds out his hand, Travis grabs it and lifts himself up. Two security guards burst in the front door. They point Tasers at Travis and Geoffrey and shout "Freeze!"

Travis fires some electricity at the security guards, knocking them unconscious. Then he grabs Geoffrey's arm and they run out the door together. They get outside and a handful of security guards are running towards them. They run the opposite direction, headed for the ocean. They reach a cliff and dive off.

Travis and Geoffrey swim back to the port. When they get there cops have arrived and are inspecting ships. Travis and Geoffrey stay hidden, poking their heads underwater any time someone points a light their way. Soon enough, the cops leave. Geoffrey points to a specific ship and the two of them swim over to it. They climb onto the ship and lay on the deck.

"You alright?"

"Ocean water doesn't feel good in open wounds, but I'm not dead or anything."

"What time is it?"

Travis pulls a smart phone out of his pocket and looks at it.

"Nearly five."

"Good. He'll be here soon."

"Who?"

They hear footsteps and lift their heads in in time to see a gruff, scruffy, chubby and bald middle-aged man board the ship.

"Hey Paul."

"Should I even ask?"

"It's better if you don't."

"You gonna be here all day?"

"If you don't mind."

"Just do me a favor and move to the side. Stay out of everyone's way."

"Will do."

Trevor and Geoffrey rise to their feet, move to the side of the ship and lean against the edge. They sit there silently watching as the crew fills the ship, every one of them stopping to say hi to Geoffrey.

"So why are we here?"

Geoffrey shrugs.

"I don't know. Just felt like a good place to be."

Travis chuckles, then contemplates for a moment.

"If I told you I could show you a world beyond this one, would you be interested?"

"I'd be curious."

As the ship departs Travis pulls out the smartphone again and pushes some buttons.

"Well then, this is definitely the place to be."

"What is that anyway?"

"This? It's my cell."

"A cell? What's that mean?"

"It's a mobile phone."

"That thing? But it's so small. You can actually call people on that?"

"Most people just text. Or tweet. Or gram. Or snap."

"Are you still speaking English?"

Travis laughs.

"The world changes a lot in 30 years."

"And it still works after you swim through the ocean? That's some amazing technology."

"Normal ones don't. This one was given to me by a god."

"God gave you a cell phone?"

"Not God, a god."

"There's only one God."

Travis chuckles.

"Actually, there's a ton of them."

He slides the phone back in his pocket.

"What humans refer to as God, Allah, Jesus, whatever name they're given, are all incorporeal beings with powers beyond the scope of human understanding."

"So you're saying all religions are wrong?"

"Actually…they're all right. The only thing they don't get correct is thinking there's only one god."

"And you've actually met one of these gods?"

"I have."

Travis turns to look at the ocean.

"And you can too."

Geoffrey follows Travis's gaze and sees the water churning. Before his eyes a whirlpool forms. Travis pats Geoffrey on the back.

"That's your red pill."

Travis lifts himself onto the edge of the ship.

"The path is before you. Decide quickly whether or not you'll follow it."

Travis jumps into the water.

"Man overboard!"

A handful of people rush to the side of the ship. They see Travis swimming away and are all perplexed. Then they see the whirlpool he's swimming towards and their curiosity is swiftly transformed to fear. They all return to their stations and start steering the ship away from the whirlpool.

"You can't just leave him out there."

"He made his choice. My first responsibility is to protect my crew."

Geoffrey runs to the side of the ship and sees Travis entering the whirlpool. Geoffrey looks back at the crew. He bites his lip then stands on the ledge.

"Geoffrey! Don't! He's already gone! You can't help him!"

Geoffrey takes a breath and dives into the water. Someone shouts "Man overboard!" and throws Geoffrey a life saver. Geoffrey ignores it and swims towards the whirlpool. He reaches it just as Travis gets pulled under the water.

"Shit!"

Geoffrey turns and tries to swim away but the current is too strong. He's being pulled in. He's desperately struggling to no avail. He keeps spinning around, moving closer and closer to the center of the vortex.

"Don't fight it."

It was a faint whisper. It sounded like Travis. Geoffrey takes a deep breath, relaxes his body and allows himself to be pulled under. The moment he submerges he begins swimming toward the surface. The he notices something strange…he can see.

His vision is perfectly clear. He can see for miles. Even stranger, there's not a single sign of aquatic life. Not a single fish, dolphin, turtle, shark or whale in sight. He lifts his head and cannot find the whirlpool. The water above his head is completely still. He doesn't see any sign of the ship. Not even a shadow.

A thought crosses Geoffrey's mind…how long has he been holding his breath? His lungs should be on fire by now. He inhales. His lungs should have filled with water. He should be gagging for air. Instead, it felt like a fresh breath of oxygen entered his lungs.

He remembers that he came here looking for Travis. He spins around and sees no sign of him. He stops to think. He's look all around. He's looked up…he hasn't looked down. He looks below and sees a pair of legs disappearing into the darkness of the depths.

Geoff starts down, diving further and further until he's enveloped by the darkness. Geoffrey no longer feels wet. It feels like he's surrounded by air. It starts feeling like that air is rushing past him. He realizes he's falling. Things starts getting brighter. He sees…white. White above him, white beneath him, white all around him. It's a familiar shade he can't quite name.

He feels himself falling faster and faster. The scenery clears. He looks beneath him and sees…white. Is that a cloud? He looks above and it's identical. Did he just fall through a cloud? Clouds beneath him, clouds above him, both stretching out further than his eyes can see. How did he get so high in the sky? Wasn't he just underwater? Geoffrey falls into the clouds beneath him.

There's a dark world filled with nothing but dry dessert sand. The skies filled with dark clouds, thunder and lightning constantly echoing. A brown hand pops up through the sand, followed by another. The two hands push against the ground and Travis rises out of the ground. All the cuts on his body are gone. He's wearing different clothes, blue jeans and a t-shirt.

"I'll never get used to that."

He brushes the sand off his body then looks around. He notices a bump on the ground and bends down. He brushes sand away until he sees a hand. He grabs it and pulls, yanking Geoffrey up through the sand.

"What the hell was that?"

"You have to be purified before you can meet the god."

"The god? It's here?"

Travis points off in the distance. There's a pedestal. A white column rising out of the sand, stopping at waist height. On top of the column rest a purple satin pillow with gold stitching. On top of that pillow rest an orb. It's a perfect circle, completely clear. Bolts of lightning keep moving around inside. They walk up to it.

"That's it?"

"Yup."

"Your god looks like a plasma ball."

"I do not look like anything. I have no natural physical body. This is the form I choose to take when I present myself to you. Most humans feel discomfort when conversing with an entity their eyes cannot behold."

The voice was booming yet gentle. It didn't seem to come from anywhere. It simply appeared in Geoffrey's brain and filled his head with its echo.

"Holy shit it can talk!"

"No. I have no voice. I implant the desires I wish to convey into your mind. Your brain waves interpret those signals into your native language."

"What are you?"

"I am a being which your species has deemed gods."

"So, which god are you? What do I call you?"

"My true name is incomprehensible to your limited mind."

"So what do I call you?"

"Such trivial matters are inconsequential. You may refer to me however you wish. I will always know when you are speaking to or about me."

"This is making less and less sense. I mean, what are you? Where did you come from? Did you build the universe?"

"Enough. I know you humans are a naturally inquisitive species. It might be your greatest trait. However, it is unnecessary at the moment. You only need to know one thing. I have powers far beyond anything you could imagine.

If you fear the danger, turn around and walk away. You will fall through the sand and wake up in your bed with no memory of the past 24 hours. If you choose adventure, place your hand atop the orb."

Geoffrey looks at Travis. He's staring back at Geoffrey with a blank expression. Geoffrey wishes he could have some sort of hint. Will any of this be worth it? He looks back to the orb. This might be the only chance he has of ever leaving Morning Dew. Can he really let this pass him by? He steps forward, holds out his hand and gently places it on the orb.

The Marina

OTHER BOOKS BY
NATHAN LYLE CUNNINGHAM

Series #1 | TOXIC – *Before the Beginning*

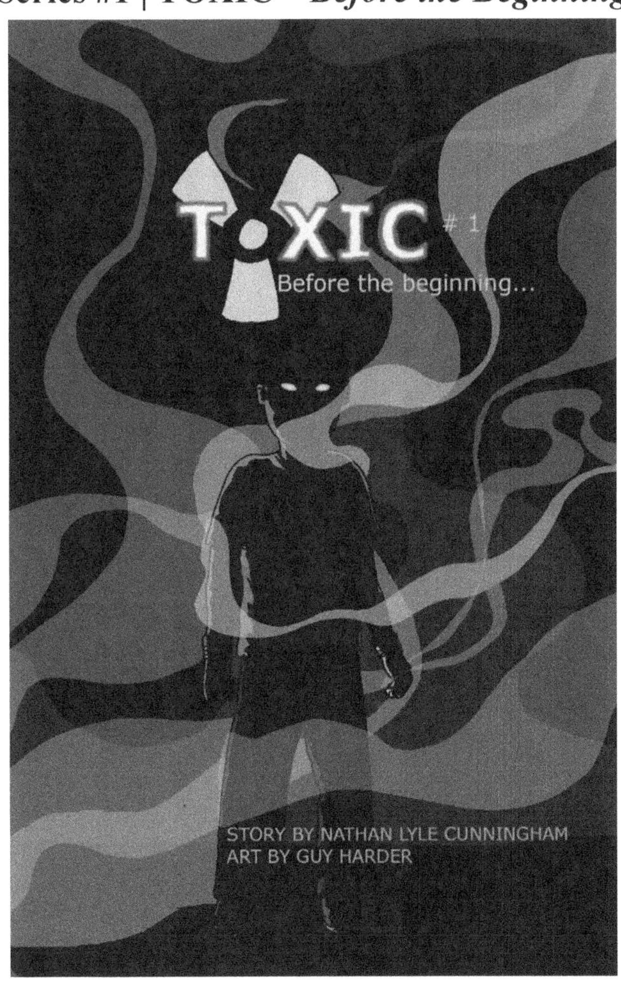

Series #2 | TOXIC

COMIC BOOK SERIES about Oscar Mireles, a boy from a town that was overrun with radiation. While more than half the town died somehow Oscar was infused with radiation. An accident that took many lives gave Oscar the power to save some. It gave him a great power, but it's also a great curse.

Everything Is Impossible

I was physically abused at home. I was picked on and beaten up at school. I tried to kill myself every year of high school. I ran away as a teenager. I was homeless for two years. Somewhere in the middle of all this I found a dream worth chasing. This is the story of my life in my own words.

Forever. Amen

In *Forever. Amen.* five friends take turns detailing the most painful months of their lives: when a dear friend is diagnosed with cancer and they struggle to come to terms with her impending death.

Nathan Lyle Cunningham
www.YouTube.com/NathanLyleOfficial
www.Twitter.com/NathanLyle